Praise for *Lo*

From a journalist who covered the January 6th attack on the U.S. Capitol:

I try to shield my 10 nieces and nephews from today's nasty politics as much as possible, in part, because today's politicians care about winning at all costs. But losing is a part of the DNA of any democracy — or it should be. "Losing is Democratic" by Kitty Felde is a fun, adventure-filled lesson for the next generation about the pitfalls of pride and heroism of humility.

—Matt Laslo, veteran congressional correspondent and lecturer at Johns Hopkins University

* * *

From Kids at Malcolm X Elementary School on Capitol Hill and Atwater Dual Language Elementary School in Los Angeles:

I can't believe this event happened, right in our backyard!

—Rubio, 4th grader, Malcolm X Elementary

It's a good way to learn about January 6th. And I liked the mystery.

—Sasha, 4th grader, Atwater Elementary

Fina is my hero!

—Amiah, 4th grader, Malcolm X Elementary

I really liked it because it teaches people about history, but it is also funny.

—Julieta, 3rd grader, Atwater Elementary

This is a good book to learn about how elections work. Also, a good way to learn about good sportsmanship.

—Oliver, 4th grader Atwater Elementary

I really enjoyed reading this book together with a friend. We learned so much by asking each other questions.

—Kaylin and Talaura, 3rd graders, Malcolm X Elementary

The book was good. I liked how the grandma was cooking carnitas! Also I like the topic of good sportsmanship and January 6th.

—Isai, 4th grader, Atwater Elementary

This book encouraged me to watch the news more with my family.

—Shamar, 4th grader, Malcolm X Elementary

This story has histories and mysteries.

—Michael, 4th grader, Atwater Elementary

I love reading about Fina's adventures - I can't wait until her next investigation!

—Josh, 4th grader, Malcolm X Elementary

Losing is Democratic

How to Talk to Kids
About January 6th

Kitty Felde

Chesapeake Press
Culver City, California

CHESAPEAKE
PRESS

Chesapeake Press
9942 Culver Blvd. Suite 1141
Culver City, CA 90232
www.chesapeakepress.org

Losing is Democratic: How to Talk to Kids
About January 6th / Kitty Felde
ISBN 979-8-9894934-4-9 (paperback)
ISBN 979-8-9894934-5-6 (e-book)
LCCN 2024912379

Cover design: Mindy R. Stein
Interior design: Kelly Wilson Samojlik

Librarians and educators, for a variety of free resources and teaching
tools including Teacher's Guides and a free podcast and "Facts Behind
the Fiction" blog, please visit our website: www.chesapeakepress.org.

This is a work of fiction based on the events of January 6, 2021.
Names, places, characters, businesses, and incidents are
products of the author's imagination or are used fictionally.

Printed in the U.S.A.

Also by Kitty Felde

THE FINA MENDOZA MYSTERIES
Book 1 – *Welcome to Washington Fina Mendoza*
Book 2 – *State of the Union*
Book 3 – *Snake in the Grass* (Spring 2025)

Podcast – The Fina Mendoza Mysteries

Available in Spanish:

LOS MISTERIOS DE FINA MENDOZA
Book 1 – *Bienvenida a Washington Fina Mendoza*
Book 2 – *Estado de la Unión*
Book 3 – *Serpiente en la Hierba* (Autumn 2025)

Democracy is on trial in the world, on a more colossal scale than ever before.

— CHARLES FLETCHER DOLE, 1906

Author's Note

I covered Capitol Hill for public radio for nearly a decade. The basement of the U.S. Capitol was my office.

On the afternoon of January 6, 2021, I was at home in California, watching the election certification vote on CNN. The violence that erupted after a rally at the White House shocked me. My office, the U.S. Capitol, was overrun by unhappy voters who wanted a different outcome to the election. Staffers and politicians, even the snack bar workers, ran for their lives.

I thought about the children whose parents worked in that building. And children who watched on TV. How do we explain the events of January 6th to them without scaring them to death? What's the bigger picture?

Losing is Democratic: How To Talk to Kids About January 6th is my way of answering those questions and inspiring hope in our next generation of citizens, encouraging them to compete fairly, win or lose graciously, and build a better, kinder, happier America for all.

Chapter One

They were building something outside the U.S. Capitol.

Papa said it's for the inauguration later this month when they swear in the new president. He said the swearing wasn't the bad kind of swearing where my grandmother made me go to confession, but a kind of promise the president made to the country, promising to "faithfully execute the Office of President of the United States" and to "protect and defend the Constitution of the United States."

Papa knew this kind of stuff because he worked inside the U.S. Capitol, as a congressman from California's 34th Congressional district.

He still went to work every day on Capitol Hill, but because of Covid, I went to school at home, sitting in front of my computer. It was pretty boring. I couldn't even do my afterschool job, walking congressional dogs. Covid also meant that I hadn't been solving any mysteries. That was my other job: Capitol Hill detective. I solved the mystery of the Demon Cat and other things. But now, it seemed like all I did was stare at my computer screen.

Chapter Two

I looked at the clock. Five more minutes until we could sign off from Zoom and say goodbye to school. I actually liked school. Except for math.

"And just a reminder, fourth graders," said our teacher Ms. Greenwood. "Your report on whichever state you chose is due tomorrow. Does anyone have any questions about the assignment? Margaret?"

We could see Margaret talking, but nothing came out of her mouth.

"Unmute, Margaret," said Ms. Greenwood.

Becka, my least favorite person in the world, rolled her eyes. "Again?"

Margaret found the unmute button. "Got it. Sorry. I picked Alaska, Ms. Greenwood."

"That's great, Margaret."

Of course Becka had something to say. "I chose North Dakota because it's the only state I haven't visited. At least not yet. I've already been to the other 49."

I almost rolled my own eyes, but I didn't.

"Good for you, Becka," said Ms. Greenwood.

"Is it okay that I picked D.C., Ms. Greenwood?" asked Michael. He was one of the school crossing guards and maybe my best friend at St. Philip. "I know it's not a state," he said. "At least not yet. But it's where we live."

"That's fine, Michael," said Ms. Greenwood.

"Did you know that Alexandria, Virginia used to be part of D.C.?" he added.

"Why don't you save the details for when we make our reports. Mason, what did you choose?"

I noticed that Mason had turned his camera off. He was probably playing video games instead of paying attention to school.

"I – uh. I'm still deciding, Ms. Greenwood," he said. "There's so many great states to choose from."

Ms. Greenwood sounded like she thought he was playing video games, too. "You'd better pick one soon, Mason. Reports are due tomorrow. What about you, Fina?"

I already knew which state I was going to write about. "I picked California, Ms. Greenwood. Where I was born."

"Very good," said Ms. Greenwood. "Now. For the news I know all of you have been waiting for: the winner of the St. Philip's reading competition between our fourth grade class and Mr. Thursby's fifth grade class."

That woke everybody up. For the past month, our class had been reading as many books as possible, trying to out-read the fifth graders. Ms. Greenwood kept track of our pages, posting the number every day in the chat box on Zoom. I picked the fattest books I could find and spent at least one hour every day reading. I did not want the fifth grade to win. Everybody else in class had been reading lots and lots of pages, too. We were sure that the fourth grade was going to win.

"And the winner is..." began Ms. Greenwood. "Well, unfortunately, it's not us. Our class read 623 pages. The fifth grade read 849 pages."

There was a groan from every little box on Zoom. Mason muttered, "No fair."

"I know, I know. It's disappointing," said Ms. Greenwood. "But just think of all the books you've read this month!"

"But we don't get the free pizza," said Margaret. "They do."

"It's a rip-off," said Mason. "And how do we know they really read all those pages? How do we know they aren't lying?"

Becka responded even before Ms. Greenwood. "How do we know *you* weren't lying about the number of pages *you* read, Mason?"

"All right. That's enough," said Ms. Greenwood.

Everybody got pretty cranky after Zooming all day, even Ms. Greenwood.

"I look forward to hearing your state reports

tomorrow. I'll see you promptly at 8:30. Try to log on early so we don't waste time. Have a good afternoon."

Chapter Three

I was trying to find things about California that might impress the kids in my class. Most of them grew up around Washington, D.C. and only knew California from TV shows. I had to explain several times that we didn't live at the beach and we didn't run into movie stars at the grocery store. Nobody believed me.

Maybe they'd be impressed by something Washingtonian.

"California," I typed into the laptop. "Home of two presidents of the United States: Richard Nixon and Ronald Reagan. And now, it is home of two vice presidents of the United States, Richard Nixon and..."

I stopped typing. That noise! It was hard to concentrate. It sounded like a duck being tortured right outside my door.

"Gabby!" I shouted.

My sister Gabby was in the high school marching band. She played clarinet. But not very well. In fact, she was pretty awful. I think they only let her in the band because they needed more clarinets. Even bad clarinets.

Today, Gabby was practicing, playing the same thing over and over again. It was some patriotic song they always played when they shot off fireworks. Fireworks gave me a headache. Gabby's music gave me one, too.

"Gabby!" I called. "I'm trying to do homework."

"And I've got pandemic band practice."

That meant she was on Zoom, wearing headphones, playing along with all the other band members who were also playing into their screens.

"Go down to the basement."

"I can't," she said. "The wifi is terrible down there."

I was going to complain to Abuelita, but the phone rang. And rang.

"Fina, my hands are full of cookie dough," called my grandmother from the kitchen. "Could you please answer that?"

"Okay, Abuelita."

I ran downstairs and picked up the family phone. We have three phones: Papa's office phone, Papa's fundraising phone, and the family phone. Papa gets in trouble with the House Ethics Committee if he mixes them up. "Mendoza residence," I said.

"Fina, this is Congresswoman Mitchell's office. I have someone here who wants to talk to you." I didn't recognize the voice on the phone, but I did hear a familiar bark in the background. Senator Something!

Senator Something wasn't a real U.S. Senator. He was a dog who belonged to a congresswoman from Georgia.

"Here you go," said the staffer. Staffers were the people who worked in a congressperson's office.

Senator Something barked and barked. He was as happy to hear my voice as I was to hear his.

"Welcome back to Washington, Senator Something! How was your Christmas?"

He barked and yapped and whined. It sounded like he was complaining about everything.

"Yeah, ours was pretty quiet, too," I said.

He complained some more. When Senator Something was in a bad mood, he griped about everything.

"I know. I really miss walking you. Hey! Wait a minute."

I shouted to my grandmother in the kitchen. "Abuelita, what if Senator Something wore a mask? Could I walk him then?"

Abuelita came in, drying her hands on a dish towel. "It is not the dog I am worried about, mija. It is all the human beings you'd meet out on your walk who might have the Coronavirus. I'm sorry, Fina. Soon. We'll all get our vaccinations soon and you can see your dog again." She snapped the towel at me, trying to cheer me up, and returned to her favorite place in the world. I could smell the cookies getting toasty in the oven. Were they chocolate chip?

"Did you hear that, Senator Something?"

He barked to say he did indeed and sighed a big doggie sigh.

"I know," I said. "Soon. That's all anyone ever says."

Gabby was still making tortured clarinet noises. Senator Something howled. Gabby's clarinet must be giving him a headache, too.

"That's Gabby," I told him. "Her high school band was supposed to play for the inauguration parade. Except of course, there is no inauguration parade because of Covid. So they're making a YouTube video instead."

He howled even louder.

"I know. You should hear it in person. Let's talk later. Okay?" He barked in agreement and we hung up. My head was really starting to thump now. "Gabby!" I shouted up the stairs. "Can't you at least play something else?"

The doorbell rang and I rushed to the front door.

"Look through the peeping hole before you open it to see who it is," called Abuelita. "And make sure they are wearing a mask."

"I know, I know."

I looked through the peephole. "It's a guy wearing a mask," I shouted to Abuelita. "He's got a pizza!"

That got Gabby's attention. Her horrible music stopped in the middle of a note. "Pizza!" she said, leaning over the staircase. "Abuelita, you didn't tell me we were having pizza for dinner."

"If we are," said Abuelita from the kitchen, "I wish someone would have told me. I've had carnitas on the stove all afternoon."

Gabby ran downstairs and crowded right behind me as I opened the door. Standing on our doorstep was a tall kid who wasn't wearing a jacket, even though it was really cold outside. "Delivery for a Fina Mendoza," he said. Except he said "Finna" instead of "Feena." But it was pizza and it was getting cold, so I didn't correct him.

"That's me," I said. "Thanks." There was probably enough pizza for dinner and cold pizza for breakfast, too.

Abuelita appeared, purse in hand. "Here, Fina," she said. "Give the nice boy a tip."

She stuffed a five dollar bill in my hand. I gave it to the pizza guy. He looked really happy. "Thanks, ma'am!" he said. I wasn't sure whether he was calling me or Abuelita "ma'am." I shut the door.

Gabby grabbed for the box. "What kind did you get?"

"I don't know. I don't even know where it came from."

Abuelita took the box from my hands. "I'll heat it up in the oven. Back to your band practice, Gabby. And Fina, you have homework."

"Yes, Abuelita," we said.

I went back upstairs to my room and opened my "California" file on the computer. Where did I leave off? Oh, yeah. Two vice presidents from California, Richard Nixon and...

The clarinet noise was back, louder than ever. How could I think? "Gabby!" I screamed.

"What's all the yelling about?" came a voice from downstairs.

It was Papa. Gabby's music was so loud, I didn't even hear his key in the front door.

"Come see for yourself!" I called.

Papa climbed the stairs. I stuck my head out of my room. "Look!"

Gabby had set up a music stand and her tablet at the end of the upstairs hallway. Screechy notes bounced off the walls.

Papa scrunched his nose. "Ah. I see."

"I have to finish my report on California. It's due tomorrow!" I whined. I must have sounded like Senator Something.

Papa sighed. "And I have a few phone calls to make before tomorrow's vote certification." Both of us listened to the song that seemed to go on and on. "Well, band practice can't go on much longer," he said. "I hope."

"Vote certification?" I asked. "I thought they were done with the election. Aren't all the votes counted? Even that Kornacki guy who wears khakis and points to the magic board finally got to go home. Why are you counting votes, Papa?"

"We're not counting them, Fina. We're finalizing the results of the electoral college."

I knew a lot of Washington words and phrases. But I didn't know that one. "Electoral college. Like USC?"

"Not exactly," said Papa.

"I don't understand."

"Blame Alexander Hamilton," said Papa. "It was his idea. The Founding Fathers didn't think voters were smart enough to elect the president themselves. So instead, on election day when we vote, we're actually casting a ballot to tell members of the electoral college how to vote *for* us."

"That doesn't seem fair, letting someone else do the voting for us."

"It's the law of the land," said Papa. "And it would take a constitutional amendment to change it. So tomorrow, the vice president will chair a meeting of the House and Senate to officially go over the results, state by state. And if someone has an issue, the House and the Senate go away to argue about it, then come back to vote on it. It's just a ceremony. Most of the time. Hey, do I smell pizza?"

Chapter Four

The next day at Zoom school, we were listening to everybody's reports. Three people picked Virginia and two picked Maryland. That made sense, since both states were next door to D.C.

It was now Margaret's turn. "And so Hawaii became the 50th state on August 21, 1959. It's called the aloha state. Aloha means goodbye *and* hello and it's the only state made out of islands. The end."

"Well done, Margaret. Thank you," said Ms. Greenwood.

"You're welcome," said Margaret. "And as soon as the pandemic ends, I want to go there!"

"You and me both, Margaret. Who's next? Mason? Camera on, Mason. You know the rules."

"Yes, Ms. Greenwood." Mason turned on his camera, but all we could see was a poster on his wall for some superhero movie.

"We'd like to see your face, Mason, when you're presenting your report."

Mason's laptop jiggled all over the place, but finally, his face came on the screen.

"Which state did you choose, Mason?" she asked.

Mason wasn't looking at the screen. "I'm, uh..."

You could see that Mason hadn't done his homework. Becka didn't wait for Mason's excuse about why he wasn't ready to give his report. "I'm ready!" she said. "I've been ready since Tuesday."

Ms. Greenwood shook her head at Mason, but sighed and said, "Alright, Becka."

"First of all," said Becka, "thank you for sending the pizza, Ms. Greenwood. It was great."

"Yeah, thanks Ms. Greenwood," said Michael. And then all the kids began thanking their teacher. I just figured that the pizza was a consolation prize for at least reading 623 pages.

"Wait a minute," said Ms. Greenwood. "What pizza?"

"A great, big pepperoni pizza!" said Margaret.

"I got one, too," said Michael. "I'm not a big pepperoni fan, so I picked it off. But it was pretty good anyway."

"You could have saved it for me," said Mason. "I love pepperoni! I got sausage and mushrooms."

"Wait a minute," said Ms. Greenwood. "Did all of you get a mystery pizza last night?"

Everybody said they did.

My detective brain started working. "I wonder who sent the pizza?" I asked.

Ms. Greenwood looked confused. "It wasn't me."

"Maybe it was the raccoons," said Margaret.

Margaret was remembering the time someone broke into our school and trashed our classroom. I had solved *that* mystery. It turned out, it was a family of raccoons who ate all the snacks we'd left in our desks when Covid had shut down in-person school.

"Raccoons were the ones who messed up our classroom," said Margaret. "Maybe it's their way of telling us 'I'm sorry.'"

Ms. Greenwood wasn't convinced. "I'm not sure raccoons are smart enough to order pizza for the class."

And then a strange thing happened. One by one, everybody's cell phone started buzzing and beeping and making noise.

Ms. Greenwood was not happy. "Class, do I have to remind you of our rule? We turn off all our devices while we're in school." And then Ms. Greenwood's phone made a loud beep-beep-beep. "Wait," she said. "Just a minute. Hello? Principal Davies?"

I heard Gabby calling from the living room. "Fina! Come look at the TV!"

"I'm in class!" I said. "And so are you. You're not supposed to have the TV on during school hours."

Gabby ignored me. "Abuelita, you've gotta come see this! It's like a movie. All those people.

Look, they're climbing all over the inauguration platform in front of the Capitol."

Abuelita ran into the living room and stared at the TV screen. "Madre de Dios!"

I was still staring at my computer. Ms. Greenwood put down her phone and looked at us. It looked like she was trying to figure out what to say. "Um. Right. Um. So, class, there is some news. I know a lot of your parents work on Capitol Hill."

Becka jumped in, telling us all for the millionth time, "My mom works for Senator Farnsworth."

Then everybody had something to say. "My dad's a reporter," said Michael. "He covers Congress."

Mason said, "My mom's a Capitol policewoman."

"My dad's a congressman," I said. It seemed like everyone in class had a parent who worked in or around the U.S. Capitol.

Ms. Greenwood was trying to get everyone's attention. "Yes, yes. Listen, all of you. You know

Congress is voting today to certify the electoral votes for the presidential election."

"We know, Ms. Greenwood," said Becka, sounding bored. "We all know about the senators and congresspeople who are going to argue that the votes shouldn't count."

"Yes, well there are a number of people who want to do more than just argue," said Ms. Greenwood. "A large crowd has surrounded the Capitol. And many of those people are trying to get inside the building."

"They can't do that," I said. "Visitors have to go through the metal detectors in the Capitol Visitor Center. Unless they have a family pass. Like me." Now I was sounding braggy like Becka.

"I know, Fina," said Ms. Greenwood. "But, well..."

"Fina," called Gabby, "they broke that window near the X-ray machine. The one on the south side of the Capitol! They're inside the building. And a bunch of people are waving Confederate flags. In Statuary Hall!"

I felt a chill that started at the back of my neck and reached all the way down to my toes. "Ms. Greenwood, my Papa's in the Capitol."

"So's my dad," said Michael.

"So's my mom!" said Becka, not sounding braggy at all. She sounded scared. So did all the rest of the kids on Zoom school. Some were crying. Some looked like they were getting ready to scream.

Ms. Greenwood put her hand in front of the camera to get everyone's attention. Then she looked into the camera and said, "Take a breath. All of you." We did. In and out. "One more," she said. And once more, we all breathed in and breathed out. "Okay," she said. "How many of you are at home without an adult?"

A lot of the kids were home alone. "All right," she said. "I want all of you to check in with your parents. Right now. Anyone who can't get hold of their mom or dad or guardian, call me. Stay inside. It's going to be all right."

I closed my laptop. Slowly, I walked into the living room where Gabby and Abuelita were sitting together on the couch, holding each other. I tried not to look at the TV screen. Tried not to look at the people knocking over fences and fighting with policemen and breaking windows at the Capitol. I closed my eyes. But I couldn't block out the one thought in my head: Papa. Where was Papa?

Chapter Five

It was after dinner before we heard from Papa. Abuelita had been praying all afternoon. Gabby had been looking at social media reports from inside the Capitol. I kept calling Papa on his office phone and his fundraising phone. He wasn't answering.

Abuelita tried to make us eat the carnitas she'd made the day before. None of us were hungry.

Finally, we heard footsteps on the metal stairs and his key in the lock. All of us rushed to the front door.

"Papa, Papa!" I cried.

Gabby threw her arms around him, something she hadn't done since she officially became a teenager. "You're home, Papa. Finally! Are you okay?"

Papa hugged us all back, kissing the top of our heads. "Mijas."

Abuelita called him by his nickname. "Tutu! Gracias a Dios! I cannot tell you how many rosaries I have prayed for your safety."

He kissed his mother above her eyebrow. "I'm home now, Mama."

We untangled ourselves from Papa and he collapsed onto the couch. We followed and sat as close to him as we could, as if to remind ourselves that he was actually here, safe and sound.

"It was so scary, Papa," I told him. "The sirens and the pictures on TV. And you didn't answer your phone."

"I dropped it when the Capitol Police moved us out of the House Chamber. We were locked inside a room for hours."

"We saw you on TV, Papa," said Gabby. "You and the lady who was praying and the other one with the ugly shoes. Up in the balcony."

"It's called the House Gallery," I said, but Gabby gave me a dirty look.

"Yes, yes," Papa said calmly. "But I'm home now and I'm fine."

I wasn't so sure. He kept taking his glasses off and rubbing his nose. He looked so tired, I thought he'd fall asleep with his eyes open.

"But why, Papa? Why did those people want to hurt the Capitol? Or even hurt you?"

Papa sighed and put his glasses back on. "Do you remember that year when your Dodgers lost to the Houston Astros? And how angry you got when you found out that the Astros were stealing signs about pitches?"

I did remember. Those Astros kept beating on trash cans to tell their teammates what pitch to expect. "They were cheating, Papa."

"That's right," said Papa. "Well, for many months now, the president has been telling his fans that he was cheated in the election."

"But he wasn't, Papa!" I said.

"No, he wasn't, Fina. But the people who believed those lies became very angry."

"The Dodgers were angry," said Gabby. "But they didn't break into the Astros' ballpark and trash their locker room and steal their stuff."

"No, they didn't," said Papa. "They worked harder and played even better the next year. They not only beat the Astros, they eventually won the World Series. Fina, that's the way you're supposed to bounce back from defeat. The right way."

I thought about that. The right way. If I was an Astros fan, would I be proud of my World Series win? Or would I bury my team's souvenir tee shirt at the bottom of the dirty clothes hamper? Would I be proud of my team, no matter what?

Papa groaned as he stood up. "I've got to go change my shirt. I'm going back to the Capitol."

"Nonsense, mijo," said Abuelita. "You are staying home with your family."

"Not tonight, Mama. Wrap me up a slice of that cold pizza and I'll take it with me."

I was worried. "Why are you going back to the Capitol, Papa?"

He crouched down so that our eyes were on the same level. "I was elected to do a job, Fina.

29

Tonight, Congress is going to face down the bullies and finish our constitutional duty: voting to certify the electoral votes."

He stood up and faced Gabby and me. "Remember this night, girls," he said. "This is democracy in action."

Chapter Six

After Papa left the house to return to Capitol Hill, I remembered who else had been near the Capitol this afternoon. I called a familiar phone number.

"Congresswoman Mitchell's office." It was really late, but I figured if Papa had to come back to the Capitol to cast his vote, so did the rest of Congress. "May I help you?" asked the staffer.

"Hello. This is Fina. Is Senator Something there?"

"Just a minute."

I held my breath. Had Senator Something been hurt by the people who broke into the Capitol? Had they dognapped him? But then I heard familiar barks in the background.

"Here you go," said the staffer.

Senator Something barked and barked.

"Senator Something! Are you alright?"

He continued to bark, telling me about his terrible day.

"I was so worried about you!" I told him. "But I figured if I didn't see you on TV, you'd be okay."

He seemed to say, "Of course I'm okay!" It was good to hear him say that.

And then I remembered the pizza.

"Senator Something," I said, "there's something else. I have another mystery to solve. We had this reading competition with the fifth grade. And the prize was free pizza delivered to everybody's house for the class that read the most pages."

He barked a lot at the word pizza. Senator Something loved pizza even more than me.

"Well," I said. "They won. The fifth graders. No pizza for us."

Senator Something was sad about that.

"I know!" I said. "I read four whole books myself! But here's the mystery: even though we lost, guess what showed up at my house last night?"

Senator Something perked up. Could it be pizza?

"Exactly!" I said. "A pizza. We all thought it was from Ms. Greenwood, but she said it wasn't. You know what I think, Senator Something? I think we got the fifth grade's pizza."

He seemed to puzzle this over and barked a question.

"I don't know what happened. But I'm going to find out. I'll start by tracing the pizza back to its origins. That means where it came from. And then..."

Chapter Seven

The guy on the other end of the phone answered on the first ring. "Mario's Pizza."

"Hello," I said. "Did you deliver a pizza to 403 A Street Southeast on Monday night?"

"Why?" he asked suspiciously, "Was something wrong with it?"

"No, it was great. Sausage and mushrooms are the perfect combo. But I'm wondering whether you can tell me who placed the order."

"Sorry, kiddo," he said. I hated it when adults called me *kiddo*. "We believe in keeping our customers' personal information private."

"Yes, but, well, you see a lot of pizzas were delivered to a lot of people on Monday night and none of us can figure out who sent them."

How could I get him to tell me the information? And then I had an idea. "We want to thank them," I said in my sweetest little kid voice.

It didn't work.

"No can do, Miss," he said. "I'm sorry."

I was getting ready to say goodbye and hang up, but the Mario's Pizza guy asked, "But you liked the pizza? Yes?"

"Yes, I did," I admitted. It was good pizza. "We all did."

"Then... would you write us a review on Yelp?" he asked.

"Fina, get off the phone!" shouted Gabby from her bedroom. "I have to ask a friend about my algebra homework!"

"Gotta go," I said quickly. "Bye."

Chapter Eight

I could hear the music coming from Gabby's room all the way downstairs. Gabby liked indie rockers with names like Spike Moriarty and Allyson Pennyfeather. It could be worse. She could be into music that's all words and no tune.

I climbed the stairs and tapped on the door. She opened it and grabbed for the phone. "Close the door behind you," she said.

I did and then flopped down on the purple striped comforter.

"Hey! Don't don't mess up my bed," she barked.

"Sorry," I said, even though I wasn't sorry. "I'm stuck."

"Stuck?"

"In my investigation."

"No one knows where the pizza came from?" she asked.

"Nope. And the pizza place won't tell me who made the order."

"Why make such a big deal about it? It's just a pizza."

"But it wasn't *our* pizza," I said.

I just sat there. Gabby watched me.

"What else?" she asked. Gabby could be annoying at times, but she knew when something was bothering me. And she knew it wasn't just the pizza.

"I'm still worried about Papa," I said. "Working in the Capitol."

"He'll be okay. You saw all those National Guard guys. And the new fences around the Capitol with razor wire on top."

The Capitol was now surrounded by high, black metal fences topped with what looked like barbed wire from some World War II movie. It made me shiver. "It looks like a prison now. That makes me even more scared."

"You know they've already caught some of the people who broke into the Capitol," said Gabby, trying to make me feel better.

It didn't work. I didn't feel better. But I was curious. "How did they find them?" I asked.

"Social media!" she said, laughing. "Some of those guys posted videos of themselves under the Rotunda or did shoutouts from the Speaker's office on Instagram."

"That was pretty dumb. Like photoshopping your own wanted poster."

"The FBI's been arresting them," she said.

"Social media..." I said to myself, thinking about the stolen pizza.

"What about it?"

"Gabby, can I borrow the phone for a minute?"

"Why?" she asked.

"Please?" I begged. I had to find out about the pizza thief.

She sighed but handed over the phone. "Don't break it."

"Duh," I said, but not in a really mean voice. I started scrolling through Instagram and TikTok. And there it was! "Hah!" I said.

"What?" asked Gabby.

I took a screenshot.

"Wait till I show this to Ms. Greenwood."

Chapter Nine

It was our first day back at Zoom school. The principal decided we needed a day with our families and canceled yesterday's classes. Today, I was ready to read my report about California.

Instead, Ms. Greenwood said, "Class, we're going to postpone the rest of our presentations about the 50 states until next week. So I would advise those of you who aren't quite finished – I'm talking to you, Mason – to use your weekend wisely. Understood?"

I think we were all glad that we didn't have to spend the afternoon listening to a bunch of boring reports about Indiana and Iowa and all the rest of the "I" states.

"Now," said Ms. Greenwood. "We haven't really talked about what happened at the U.S. Capitol on Wednesday. First of all, I'm so very glad your parents are all okay. But how are you feeling?"

We were all quiet for a while, remembering that terrible day. Finally, Margaret admitted, "It was scary."

Michael was angry. "They broke my dad's TV camera. Even though he was wearing his press ID."

Even Becka was upset. "I'm so mad at those people! My mom said she had to hide in the bathroom in the back of the senator's office for five hours."

"My dad had to get fifteen stitches," said Mason, a bit quieter than usual.

Michael asked the question that all of us were thinking. "But why did it happen, Ms. Greenwood?"

Ms. Greenwood did what she often did: she asked us a question in return. "Why do you think it happened?"

We were quiet for a bit, then Margaret suggested, "Because those people didn't want to wait in line to get into the Capitol?"

"I'm afraid it was more than that, Margaret."

"Maybe they just wanted to see themselves all over social media," said Mason. "You know, be the king of TikTok."

"Interesting," said Ms. Greenwood.

I spoke up. "My Papa said it's because people were angry because their person lost the election."

Ms. Greenwood nodded her head. "Losing. Let's talk a bit about losing. And about winning. And about American history."

There were groans from nearly every Zoom screen.

"All right, all right," said Ms. Greenwood. "Let's start with something simple. You all know who the first president of the United States was."

"Duh," said Becka. "George Washington."

"Thank you, Becka. And he served how many years as president?"

"Eight," said Michael. "But they wanted him to stay president forever."

"They?" asked Ms. Greenwood.

"The people in the United States," he said. "George Washington was like a rock star."

"I suppose he was."

Mason perked up, "Now *he* was the king of TikTok. If they'd had TikTok back in the 1700's."

"But President Washington didn't want to be an American king," I said. "So he didn't run for reelection another time."

Ms. Greenwood nodded. "Yes, that's right. Now. What happened next? Yes, Margaret?"

"George Washington went home to Mount Vernon," she said.

I didn't think that was the answer Ms. Greenwood was looking for. "Well, yes, he did. But what happened to the United States? Who was the second president?"

"Sam Adams," said Mason.

"Actually," said Ms. Greenwood, "that's the beer."

"John Adams!" said Michael.

"That's right. But what happened four years later when *he* ran for reelection?"

Becka knew that answer. Of course she did. "John Adams lost. To Thomas Jefferson. Although it was actually the House of

Representatives that decided that election. Right, Ms. Greenwood?"

"You are correct, Becka," said Ms. Greenwood. "Do you think he was mad? John Adams, I mean."

"I would be," said Mason. "Especially since he thought Congress cheated him out of winning."

Michael agreed. "I think he was mad, too, Ms. Greenwood. He went right home to his farm. He didn't even stay for the inauguration of the new president."

Ms. Greenwood looked pleased that so many of us remembered so much about the first presidents. "So what does this tell us?" she asked.

"That you shouldn't run against Thomas Jefferson?"

"That's one answer, Margaret. John Adams was very angry with Thomas Jefferson for many, many years. But then something happened. The two men started writing letters to each other. 158 letters over the years."

"What did they write about?" asked Margaret.

"You name it. Politics, of course. The role of religion throughout history, the French

Revolution, how Americans were creating their own version of the English language, about growing old. They kept talking to each other, through their letters. Adams told Jefferson, 'You and I ought not to die, before we have explained ourselves to each other.'"

A hundred and fifty-eight letters! And they had to write them by hand, using those turkey feather pens. I bet their hands hurt.

"So they became friends?" asked Michael.

"I wouldn't go that far," she said. "Friendly rivals is more like it. But let's get back to the thing John Adams did after losing the election. Is there some important lesson that we can learn?"

I thought about the election that John Adams lost. And about the Houston Astros who won the World Series, but lost in a different way. And I thought about our stolen pizza and the reading competition. Was there a lesson there, too?

"That losing is important?" I suggested.

"What do you mean by that, Fina?"

"Well," I said. "It's like in Little League. After a game, the coaches make the players line up and the winners and the losers all give each other high fives."

"Good sportsmanship!" said Michael.

My brain kept working it out. "But it's more than that. Losing is important in baseball. Important in all sports. And in elections. If no one loses, no one wins. Everybody loses."

"But losing stinks," said Margaret.

"It does indeed," said Ms. Greenwood.

"Are you talking about the reading competition, Ms. Greenwood?" I asked.

"I am," she said. "Someone – and I won't say who – posted a video of him or herself on TikTok, stuffing his or her mouth with pizza and saying, 'who's a loser now, fifth grade?' At least that's what I think they said, since their mouth was full of pizza at the time."

"Our pizza?" asked Margaret.

"Yes. Or more accurately, the fifth grade's pizza."

There wasn't exactly a gasp, but everyone in class started talking at once, saying, "It wasn't me." "Not me." "I wouldn't do something like that."

"That's enough," said Ms. Greenwood, firmly. "I have spoken with the student's parents and they will reimburse the school for the cost of the pizza and we will send the reading prize to the fifth graders tonight. But our fourth grade reputation has been tarnished. How can we show our school community that we are good losers? Good citizens?"

That stumped us. What could we do?

Becka suggested, "We could just tell the fifth grade who did it."

Ms. Greenwood shook her head. "And invite mob justice? I don't think that's particularly democratic."

Michael looked thoughtful. "We could hold a class trial. And vote on a punishment."

"We could," said Ms. Greenwood. "But frankly, I think the punishment coming from this person's parents will be sufficient. What about the rest of us? What should we do?"

"But we didn't steal the pizzas," said Margaret.

"No. But we lost the reading contest. How can we show the fifth grade and the rest of St. Philip's that we are gracious losers?"

"We could give them high fives in the hall," said Margaret.

"We could apologize for eating their pizza," suggested Michael.

What could we do? And then I remembered all those letters. "I think we should write the fifth grade class a letter. All of us. Just like John Adams and Thomas Jefferson. Telling them we're sorry. And congratulations."

"Yeah," said Becka. "And challenging them to another reading competition next month!"

"Excellent!" said Ms. Greenwood. "So that will be your assignment for the weekend. Each of you will write a letter of apology to the fifth grade. And next week, we'll deliver them to Mr. Thursby for his class."

Margaret had a question. "Ms. Greenwood, do we have to write 158 letters?"

"I don't think that'll be necessary, Margaret. Just one letter is fine."

Chapter Ten

Gabby was still practicing for the inauguration YouTube performance. She didn't sound any better than last week.

I was on the phone, catching Senator Something up on the pizza case. "Can you believe it, Senator Something? It was Mason, of course. He posted that stupid video on TikTok, bragging that he got away with it. I found it and sent a link and a screenshot to Ms. Greenwood. Remember, Senator Something: you've gotta be careful with social media."

Senator Something said something that sounded like he was always careful on social media.

"Do you want to know how Mason did it?"

Senator Something barked. He loved solving mysteries.

"Mr. Thursby emailed the addresses of all the fifth graders to the pizza place when he placed the order, so they'd know where to deliver the pizzas. Mason pretended to be Mr. Thursby and emailed the pizza people the fourth grade addresses instead, saying, 'there'd been a mistake.'"

Senator Something gave a bark that sounded like a laugh.

"It's not funny, Senator Something. It costs a lot of money to send pizzas to the wrong people. And worse than that, it made the whole fourth grade class look like real losers. Like we're babies or something."

Senator Something whined an apology for laughing.

"Anyway," I said. "I solved the mystery of the missing pizza, Senator Something! What do you think our next case will be?"

Did you enjoy this book?

Please take a few moments to write a review.

Let Kitty know what you thought about
Losing is Democratic:
How to Talk to Kids about January 6th
by leaving a short review on Amazon,
Goodreads, or your favorite bookstore's website.

It will help other teachers, librarians,
parents, and children discover
the world of Fina Mendoza.

(If you're under 13, ask a
grownup to help you.)

Thank you!

Want more Fina Mendoza?

FREE educational resources are available!

- **Podcast** based on the books and current events.

- **Facts Behind the Fiction** blog and newsletter with historical context for both the books and podcast episodes.

- Downloadable 7-page curriculum for *Losing is Democratic* includes language arts, math, social studies, and social emotional leanring discussions.

- Perfect for **classroom** or **homeschooling** settings.

**Go to www.chesapeakepress.org
or use this QR code to download the
curriculum as its own PDF!**

Check out our Podcast!

THE FINA MENDOZA MYSTERIES

- **Season One:** The Mystery of the Demon Cat of Capitol Hill (8 episodes + bonus episodes)
- **Season Two:** The Mystery of Chickcharney, the Bird with the Lizard Tail (18 episodes + bonus episodes)
- **Special Episodes:**
  *January 6th: Losing is Democratic ·
  Let Kids Vote! · Fina's Coronavirus Diary*

**Plus backstories on the characters
and the actors who voice them!**

**Available FREE on Apple
Podcasts, Spotify, Audible,
Soundcloud, or wherever
you listen to podcasts.**

And Don't Forget about our Blog!

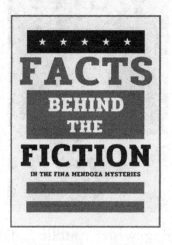

Subscribe to the "FACTS BEHIND THE
FICTION" newsletter at our website to
receive FACTS as soon as they're published!

Go to www.chesapeakepress.org.

About the Author

Award-winning writer, public radio journalist, and TEDx speaker **Kitty Felde** hosts the ***Book Club for Kids*** podcast. With more than 1.4 million downloads, the show has been named one of the top 10 kidcasts in the world by *The Times* of London.

Kitty has a remarkable talent for talking to kids and she shared her super power in a TEDx UCLA talk.

The native Angeleno created the Washington bureau for Southern California Public Radio, reporting on Congress. She's covered everything from war crimes trials to OJ Simpson to baseball, and hosted a daily talk show in Los Angeles for nearly a decade. Kitty had a front row seat at one of the January 6th Committee hearings.

She won the Los Angeles Radio *Journalist of the Year* award three times in three years from the Society of Professional Journalists and the L.A. Press Club.

As a journalist, Kitty explained how government works to grownups. Now she explains it to kids in a series of mystery novels and podcasts called ***The Fina Mendoza Mysteries***. She also writes the companion blog ***Facts Behind the Fiction***, available on the Chesapeake Press website (www.chesapeakepress.org).

Find Kitty at www.kittyfelde.com
and @kittyfelde.

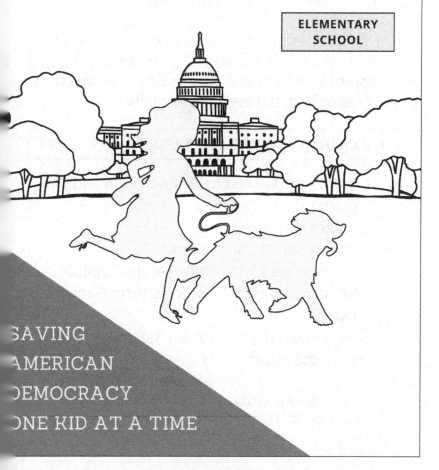

CURRICULUM

LOSING IS DEMOCRATIC: HOW TO TALK TO KIDS ABOUT JANUARY 6TH

By Kitty Felde

A Novella in The Fina Mendoza Mysteries Series
of Books and Podcasts

CHESAPEAKE
PRESS

ELEMENTARY
SCHOOL

SAVING
AMERICAN
DEMOCRACY
ONE KID AT A TIME

Kitty Felde

STORY SYNOPSIS

Ten-year-old Fina Mendoza and her fourth grade
class lose a reading competition to the fifth
grade. And yet, the promised first prize of pizza is
delivered to the homes of the entire fourth
grade. Fina is in Zoom class when the U.S. Capitol
is overrun by angry voters on January 6th. Fina's
congressman father is inside, voting to certify the
election, but returns home later to assure his
family that he is all right. He returns to vote, an
act he calls "democracy in action."

Fina decides to solve the pizza mystery. Her class
discusses the violence on Capitol Hill, putting it in
historical context and examining the importance
of losing in both baseball and politics.

READING COMPREHENSION QUESTIONS

1. What's the contest between the 4th and 5th
   grade?
2. What's the prize?
3. Who is Senator Something?
4. What is Fina's father doing at the Capitol?
5. What instrument does Fina's sister Gabby
   play?
6. How does Fina track down the person who
   stole the pizzas?

ANSWERS: 1. who can read the most pages;
2. pizza; 3. dog; 4. voting to certify the election;
5. clarinet; 6. social media

VOCABULARY, PAGE 1

- **Abuelita** (noun) - grandmother.
- **accurately** (adverb) - to do something correctly in all details.
- **Capitol Hill -** a neighborhood in Washington, D.C. near the U.S. Capitol that includes the U.S. Supreme Court building, the various buildings of the Library of Congress, and the houses nearby.
- **carnitas** (noun) – a Mexican pork dish.
- **Confederate flag** (noun) – the red flag with a blue X and white stars flown by states that broke apart from the United States. Today it is a symbol of racism.
- **consolation prize** (noun) - a prize for someone who didn't win.
- **constitutional amendment** (noun) – the way the U.S. Constitution can be changed. It takes either a two-thirds majority vote in Congress or a constitutional convention called for by two-thirds of state legislatures.
- **constitutional duty** (noun) - a job that is required to be done by the U.S. Constitution.
- **democracy** (noun) - a form of government in which the people have the authority to choose the people who govern them.
- **Dodgers/Astros** (noun) - professional baseball teams.

Kitty Felde

VOCABULARY, PAGE 2

- **Electoral College** (noun) – In other U.S. elections, candidates are elected directly by popular vote. But the president and vice president are chosen by 538 people from states across America. Each state has the same number of electors as it does members of Congress. It takes 270 electoral votes to win.
- **electoral votes (noun)** - the votes cast by the Electoral College.
- **Founding Fathers** (noun) - leaders who helped win American independence from England.
- **French Revolution** (historic event) - the violent event that ended the rule of kings and queens in France in the late 1700's.
- **good sportsmanship** (noun) - playing a game and treating your opponents with respect.
- **gracias a Dios** (Spanish phrase) - thank God.
- **House Chamber** (noun) - the large room where the House of Representatives casts votes.
- **House Gallery** (noun) - the balcony that overlooks the House Floor where members of Congress vote.
- **House of Representatives** (noun) - the 435 women and men who represent us in Congress. The other governing body is the Senate.

VOCABULARY, PAGE 3

- **inauguration** (noun) – the ceremony where the new president officially takes office.
- **Kornacki** (person) – Steve Kornacki is a political journalist famous for his electronic vote counting graphics.
- **Madre de Dios** (Spanish) - Mother of God.
- **mija/mijo (Spanish)** - a sweet way of saying my daughter/son.
- **Mt. Vernon** (noun) - the house and land in Virginia owned by George Washington.
- **National Guard** (noun) - military force based in states but also available for federal use.
- **particularly** (adverb) - specifically.
- **patriotic** (adjective) - a strong emotion for one's country.
- **promptly** (adverb) - quickly.
- **personal information** (noun) - information that can identify you.
- **postpone** (verb) - to do something later.
- **reimburse** (verb) - to repay a sum of money.
- **reputation** (noun) - the opinions and beliefs. someone has about someone or something.
- **rivals** (noun) - people who compete against each other.
- **rosaries** (noun) - a Catholic prayer tradition using a string of beads.

Kitty Felde

VOCABULARY, PAGE 4

- **Rotunda** (noun) - the round room in the middle of the U.S. Capitol, topped by a dome.
- **souvenir** (noun) - something kept as a reminder of a person, place, or event.
- **sufficient** (adjective) - enough.
- **tarnished** (verb) - dirtied.
- **vote certification** (noun) – the last step in a presidential election, when each state sends its official paperwork to Washington and Congress verifies that the results are correct.
- **World Series** (noun) - the competition that decides who has the best team in baseball.

BEFORE READING

Activate Student Knowledge
Begin the lesson by asking students to share what they know about the election process in America.

Some questions to guide discussion:
1. Who gets to vote in an election?
2. What's the electoral college?
3. What's the role of Congress in an election for president?
4. What happened on January 6, 2021 at the U.S. Capitol?
5. Why did it happen?

Preview the vocabulary by reading aloud the terms and their definitions. How do the political terms fit in with what students know about elections?

INTRODUCE THE STORY

Say to students: In this episode, Fina and her fourth grade classmates are competing in a reading competition with fifth graders. The prize is free pizza. But somehow, the pizza goes to the losers. Fina must find out what happened. Meanwhile, Fina's congressman father is voting to certify the election when the U.S. Capitol comes under attack.

Kitty Felde

AFTER READING

Reflect on the story:
Ask students to respond to the comprehension questions and share their responses with a partner, small group, or the whole class. Take time for student reflection on the story. Use the discussion questions to let students discuss their own understanding of the events of January 6, 2021, the importance of losing, and appropriate punishment for doing wrong.

READING COMPREHENSION QUESTIONS

- Why do you think people attacked the U.S. Capitol on January 6, 2021?

- Is losing important? Why?

- In the story, losing is important in baseball and politics. Where else?

- Did Mason receive the appropriate punishment? Why or why not? What would be appropriate?

- In the story, the kids use letter writing as a way to apologize. Are there other ways?

EXTERNAL MATERIALS

FOR TEACHERS/PARENTS/LIBRARIANS:

- NPR News - "How To Talk To Kids About The Riots At The U.S. Capitol"

  www.tinyurl.com/npr-talk-to-kids-about-riots

- Common Sense Media - "Talking to Kids About the Violence at the US Capitol"

  www.commonsensemedia.org/articles/talking-to-kids-about-the-violence-at-the-us-capitol

- *Education Week* - "How to Talk About Social Media and the Capitol Insurrection: A Guide for Teachers"

  www.edweek.org/teaching-learning/how-to-talk-about-social-media-and-the-capitol-insurrection-a-guide-for-teachers/2021/01

- *The Harvard Gazette* - "How to Talk to Your Kids about the Capitol Riots"

  news.harvard.edu/gazette/story/2021/01/how-to-talk-to-your-kids-about-the-capitol-riots

- *NY Daily News* - "Election workers: Superheroes in Neon Nails" by Kitty Felde

  www.tinyurl.com/ny-dn-election-workers-article

EXTERNAL MATERIALS

FOR CHILDREN:

- Podcast - "The Fina Mendoza Mysteries" special episode: *January 6th: Losing is Democratic*

  Listen here: www.chesapeakepress.org/january6th
  Recent episodes: thefinamendozamysteries.libsyn.com

- *Scholastic* News - "Chaos at the U.S. Capitol"

  junior.scholastic.com/pages/news/2020-21/
  chaos-at-the-us-capitol.html

- National Archive Info -

  What is the Electoral College?

  www.archives.gov/electoral-college/about

  Peaceful Transition of Power

  www.archives.gov/publications/
  prologue/2000/winter/inaugurations

- *The Washington Post* Newspaper Column - "In Politics, as in Sports, if the Final Score isn't Accepted, the Whole Game is Lost"

  www.washingtonpost.com/sports/2020/12/04/
  sports-elections-cheating-world-series

LITURATURE CONNECTIONS

- *Welcome to Washington Fina Mendoza* by Kitty Felde
- *Teacher's Guide to Welcome to Washington Fina Mendoza* by Kitty Felde
- *State of the Union: A Fina Mendoza Mystery* by Kitty Felde
- *Teacher's Guide to State of the Union* by F. Linda Marks
- *The January 6th Report: The Report of the Select Committee to Investigate the January 6th Attack on the United States Capitol*

FACTS BEHIND THE FICTION

The Fina Mendoza Mysteries are fiction, but there are LOTS of facts about Congress, the US Capitol, and civics in general packed in every book chapter and every podcast episode.

The **"Facts Behind the Fiction"** blog is published about once a month and includes historical context related to current events and topics appearing in The Fina Mendoza Mysteries.

Subscribe to our newsletter to receive FACTS as soon as they're published and you'll receive a link to download this curriculum as its own PDF.

www.subscribepage.com/lid

A FINA MENDOZA MYSTERY

Welcome to
Washington
Fina Mendoza

KITTY FELDE

Here's a sneak preview of Fina's first adventure!

Welcome to Washington Fina Mendoza

Book 1 of
The Fina Mendoza Mysteries

Chapter One

"There's no such thing as a Demon Cat of Capitol Hill."

That was what Papa would say, and he should know. Papa's a big deal congressman, the smartest person in Washington, D.C. But Papa wasn't down here in the Crypt. Nobody was here but me and a circle of statues, all of them Founding Fathers I'd never heard of from states I'd never visited. Like Caesar Rodney from Delaware, a guy who signed the Declaration of Independence who scowled at me from across the room. I felt those marble eyes staring as if they were saying, "You wouldn't even be in the Crypt after visiting hours, Fina Mendoza, if you hadn't lost your school sweatshirt. Again."

The Crypt wasn't a friendly room. It might be convenient, smack in the middle of the Capitol building with doorways leading everywhere. But it wasn't a place that invited you to stick around and make yourself comfortable. Stone floors and stone columns made it a cold place. During the day, it was crowded with school groups, kids wearing matching neon green tee shirts. Those kids ignored the tour guides and made fun of the exhibits. They never looked at the ancient wooden clock from the old House chamber. They walked right past the replica of the Magna Carta inside its giant plastic box.

The one thing they did like was the miniature model of the National Mall. It was one of the few things in the Capitol that you could touch without getting yelled at. Tiny white plastic versions of the Lincoln Memorial and the U.S. Capitol sat at opposite ends on top of a long table. In between, there were miniature memorials and monuments and museums on the Mall. It was my favorite thing in the Capitol, too.

That was why I had come to the Crypt this afternoon. I wanted to memorize every building on the National Mall so that I would know as much about Washington as Papa. The table was just my height. I could look from one end of the Mall to the other without standing on tiptoe.

Of course, there was another reason I was in the Capitol Crypt: I had no place else to go. My sister Gabby had band practice, marching around her high school football field with a clarinet. My grandmother was coming east to take care of us, but not for another two weeks. Until then, I had to come straight to the Capitol after school and wait until Papa finished working. Papa said I could go over to a friend's house to do homework. But after a month at my new school, I still didn't have a single new friend.

So I came to the Crypt, to study the model of the National Mall. There was something weird about it. There were two Washington Monuments right in the middle. I don't know why. I wanted to ask Papa about it. But first, I had to find my sweatshirt.

I started my search by circling the room, ignoring those Founding Fathers watching my every move. The Crypt was dark and echoey in the late afternoon. Strange shadows painted the arched ceiling. The ancient air conditioner wheezed as if it was about to die at any moment. The Crypt never felt scary in the middle of the day when tour guides in red jackets used their outside voices, warning kids not to lean on the display cases. Now, all those bored eighth graders were back on buses, going home to Pennsylvania or Delaware or New Jersey. All the tour guides had traded in their official red jackets for overcoats and scarves and were heading to the Metro. It was just me here in the Crypt. Me...and something else.

I felt a tingling behind my ears, a sense that I wasn't alone. I looked behind me. Nothing was there. "Hello?" I said, trying not to squeak. There was no answer.

The saucer-shaped ceiling lights were turned down low. Anything could be hiding behind the fat columns. Anything. My navy fleece wasn't here, but something else was.

I tried again. "Hello?"

Don't be a baby, Fina, I told myself. You're ten years old now. Or "double digits" as my sister Gabby called it. You're too old to be afraid of the dark. Don't be a scaredy-cat. I tried to stand a little bit taller, but that was hard to do when you're shorter than everybody else in fourth grade. "Hello? Anybody there?" I asked.

That was when I heard it: a soft, bouncy sound, like a marshmallow dropped on the kitchen floor. I knew there were no marshmallows in the Crypt. Papa said there weren't any dead bodies, either, even though that was what you were supposed to put in a Crypt. Papa said Congress wanted to bury George Washington here, but Martha wanted the President home with her at Mt. Vernon.

But what if George Washington wanted to be buried in the Crypt? What if his ghost had come back to haunt the place? Maybe he waited until all the tourists were gone and the only person left in the Crypt was the girl who forgot where she left her hoodie and he was going to—

That was when I saw it. A ginormous shadow

crept up the wall. It was tall and curved, like a ghostly question mark. The shadow quivered in the air. There was a howl, a long, whiny "mrreowow." It seemed to ask, "Fina Mendoza, what are you doing here?"

"My sweatshirt," I said, my voice cracking.

The ghost mrreowowed again, seeming to echo, "Sweatshirt?"

It was just a stupid school sweatshirt. If it was lost forever, Gabby would yell at me about being irresponsible, and Papa would make me use my birthday money to buy a new one. That was pretty bad, but was it worse than having the ghost of George Washington mad at me? His face looked so serious on the front of a one dollar bill, like he thought I was wasting money on something stupid. Now he wanted to know why I was in the Crypt.

"I'm sorry," I whispered to the ghost. "I'm sorry. I'll just leave now."

Before I could escape, something moved. It was silent. It was swift. Behind the statue of Caesar Rodney, I saw a swish of something black, like a backpack with feet or a garbage bag with a tail. I opened my mouth to scream, but nothing came out. I told my feet to start running, but they weren't listening.

I saw a flash of yellow eyes and the flick of a furry tail. What was it? It wasn't the ghost of George Washington. It was much more real, much more scary.

As quickly as the creature appeared, it was gone.

I unstuck my feet and hurried over to look behind Caesar Rodney's marble boot, just to be sure. What had I just seen? Where had it come from? Where had it gone? Was it real? Or had I imagined the whole thing?

I listened again. This time, I heard squeaky footsteps, rubber-bottomed shoes on the stone floors.

"Still here, kid?"

It was that Capitol Policewoman. The one who yelled at me for not taking off my seven jangly bracelets before walking through the metal detector.

"I–I thought I heard something."

"It's an old building. You hear lots of things," she said.

"Like an animal. An angry creature."

"Ah," she said, and her voice got lower. "The Demon Cat. You have heard of the Demon Cat, haven't you?"

I didn't answer. I hadn't heard of any Demon Cat and didn't want to waste my time listening to some stupid story. Besides, the creature I saw was bigger than a cat. Much bigger.

"The rumor is..."

Oh, boy, I thought. Here it comes.

The policewoman leaned in and whispered. "Occasionally, people will see a black cat that swells to the size of a Mini Cooper, eyes glowing, hissing and spitting."

The creature I saw wasn't quite the size of a small car, but it was black. "Does it yowl?" I didn't mean to ask that, but it just popped out of my mouth. The Capitol policewoman nodded grimly. "It usually makes an appearance right before something really bad happens."

My heart started to beat loudly. I knew that really bad things happened to people. They had happened to me, to the whole Mendoza family, back in California. Moving to Washington was supposed to get Gabby and me away from all the bad things. I didn't want to think about really bad things right now. My voice got very quiet. "How bad?"

The policewoman shrugged. "Depends. A lawmaker loses an election."

I breathed a sigh of relief. Big deal, I thought. I wasn't a member of Congress. And Papa won his last election by a zillion votes.

"Or bad luck follows you wherever you go," she said, "like the tail of the Demon Cat."

I knew I shouldn't believe her, but I felt a shiver at the top of my neck that traveled down my whole back. The Mendoza family didn't need any more bad luck.

"Or someone could even die," she whispered.

I gasped.

"Beware the curse," she said. "The curse of the Demon Cat of Capitol Hill."

I slowly backed away from her until I got to one of the stone archways. Forget the sweatshirt! I turned and ran down the long, dark hallway to reach the elevator. I could still hear her voice in my head, saying over and over again, "Beware the curse, the curse of the Demon Cat."

Read more in
Welcome to Washington Fina Mendoza
by Kitty Felde!